KICKER

orca sports

KICKER

MICHELE MARTIN BOSSLEY

ORCA BOOK PUBLISHERS

Library and Archives Canada Cataloguing in Publication

Bossley, Michele Martin
Kicker / written by Michele Martin Bossley.
(Orca sports)

ISBN 978-1-55143-706-4

I. Title. II. Series.
PS8553.O7394K53 2007   JC813'.54   C2006-907028-8

Summary: When electronic threats and sabotage seem set to derail
the soccer season, Izzy and Julia have to find out the truth.

*Orca Book Publishers is dedicated to preserving the environment and has printed
this book on paper certified by the Forest Stewardship Council®.*

First published in the United States, 2007
Library of Congress Control Number: 2006940589

Orca Book Publishers gratefully acknowledges the support for its publishing
programs provided by the following agencies: the Government of Canada
through the Canada Book Fund and the Canada Council for the Arts,
and the Province of British Columbia through the BC Arts Council
and the Book Publishing Tax Credit.

Cover photography by Getty Images

ORCA BOOK PUBLISHERS
PO Box 5626, Stn. B
Victoria, BC Canada
V8R 6S4

ORCA BOOK PUBLISHERS
PO Box 468
Custer, WA USA
98240-0468

www.orcabook.com
Printed and bound in Canada.

15 14 13 12 • 7 6 5 4

For Mike, with love.

Author's Note

Izzy's story is completely fiction, but I have based some parts on a real event. There really was a train robbery that took place in the Crowsnest Pass area of Alberta, Canada in 1920. While I have fictionalized the name of one of the robbers (Richard Ausby) and his family's homestead for my story, as well as the value and extent of the loot, information about the Bellevue Café shootout was taken from the Wikipedia entry on Bellevue, Alberta. It is used here, in a modified format, under the terms of the GNU Free Documentation License, Version 1.2 or any later version published by the Free Software Foundation. The page is located at http://en.wikipedia.org/wiki/Special: Search/Bellevue_Alberta.

chapter one

"Izzy! Take the shot!" my coach hollered from the sidelines. I deked sideways to avoid the sweeper on the other team and focused on the upper left corner of the goal.

Please, I thought. Let me do it this time. My stomach tightened. I drew back my foot and kicked the ball. It skittered sideways, heading right for the sweeper. Desperate, I scrambled forward and kicked the ball again toward the net.

The goalie blocked it. I heard the sound of leather smacking skin as the ball hit her thigh, just below the hem of her shorts.

The goalie winced and dove for the loose ball, but it was too late.

Julia, our star player, raced in for the rebound and blasted the ball into the net.

Goal!

Our team cheered, leaving me and the beaten goalie with sour looks on our faces. Not that I wasn't happy to have the goal. It's just that Julia—who also happens to be my best friend—gets all the fanfare while, when it really counts, I seem to botch every shot. Never mind the fact that I just got an assist. Jules is our star, and anything she does is met with applause.

"Are you ever going to quit hogging the ball?" I grumbled to her on the bench. Our team's next shift took the field.

"Nope." Julia teased, taking a swig of water and swishing it around in her mouth.

"You've been doing this to me since we were eight." I adjusted the laces on one of my cleats and retied the knot. "I set you up for the perfect shot, you score, everyone thinks you're terrific, and then you don't even say thank you."

Julia fastened her big blue eyes on me and smiled sweetly. "Thank you."

"It doesn't count now," I told her. "I just told you to say it."

"It still counts if I mean it," said Julia.

"You don't," I said.

"I do too." Julia's gaze turned to the field. "Besides, you should be happy. We're winning."

"We're always winning," I answered. I had my curly brown hair braided back, but I could feel the elastic coming loose. I quickly retied it as our coach, Dan Collins, walked up.

"Don't count your chickens, ladies." He'd overheard my last remark. "Izzy, I want you to watch your footwork out there. This isn't a cattle stampede. You'll find more chances to pass if you finesse around the opposition. Julia, keep your head up, mark your man."

"Girl," Julia corrected.

"You're very good at game strategy. Keep it up," Coach said.

He glanced at his watch. "Should be nearly time to switch shifts. Get ready." He moved off down the line.

I pulled up my socks and took a last gulp of water. Then I chewed on a hangnail, waiting for the coach's signal.

Julia watched me. "Why are you so nervous, Iz?"

I put my hand in my lap. "I'm not."

"You are so."

I opened my mouth to explain, but just then Coach motioned for a shift change.

"Come on." Julia jumped up.

I raced after her and took my position. I usually played midfield, but today Coach had me up as a forward. Julia played striker, which was the center forward. The striker was usually the player with the best opportunities to score, and Julia made the most of every single one.

Julia and I have been friends since we started playing soccer together when we were eight. We didn't always get to play on the same team, but we go to the same school as well, so we always hung out together. I can't even remember when she wasn't my best friend.

Julia snagged the ball from the other team's forward and began to work her way down the field. I kept pace with her, waiting to support the play. She didn't need it. She maneuvered around player after player, and then she looked straight at me, dashed ahead and passed back to me.

"Go for it, Iz!" she yelled.

I took the ball and dribbled up the sideline. Three players were blocking me—they had materialized from nowhere—and I couldn't get through. Then I remembered Coach's advice.

Finesse. Don't bulldoze.

I shifted the ball from foot to foot— backward, forward, side-to-side. I turned. I twisted. I began to feel as though I was dancing a ballet in *Swan Lake*.

But it worked! I wormed through the barrier. There was only the goalie to contend with now.

She faced me grimly, probably remembering the nasty welt I'd left on her leg the last time

I'd approached. This time her gloved hands were outstretched, ready for the hefty thump she was sure was coming.

Instead, I chose a deft delivery, something with a little more skill. And as I wound up to kick the ball, in a beautiful position to score a goal, someone snagged the ball from behind me. The other defenseman shot forward and belted the ball, a swirl of black and white, back down the field.

So much for finesse.

"Nice try, Iz," Julia called back as she raced down the field after the ball. I shook my head and followed her.

I didn't get another chance to score during that shift. Instead, the other team out-passed us, leaving me gasping and breathless by the time our shift was called off.

"Girls! You can't let them play keep-away with you," Coach said as we came to the bench. "If they start passing the ball around, you have to mark your man. That's the only way we'll get possession. Otherwise they'll just run you down, get you too tired, and then they'll have us."

I dropped onto the bench in relief. "Are we still winning?" I groaned.

"By one point," said Julia. She was red-faced and sweating too. Her pale blond hair escaped in straggling wisps from her ponytail and stuck to her forehead.

"Good." I craned my neck to see around some of my teammates. "Nicola, could you please move?"

Taller than the rest of the girls on our team, Nicola shot me an annoyed look, like I was trying to insult her. "Why?"

"I'm looking for someone."

"Who?" Julia doused her face with a squirt from the water bottle.

"Remember when you asked me why I was so nervous? Well, I think that must be a scout over there."

"A what?" Julia said.

"A scout. As in for the national team." I jerked my head toward a man who was standing near the sidelines, wearing a shirt and tie. His light brown hair was streaked with artificial blond, and his face was evenly tanned to a rich color. He looked like he spent a lot of time in the tanning salon. Expensive sunglasses were propped on top of his head, a cell phone dangled from a hip holster. He stood a little away from the crowd, squinting at the wooded area in the distance, beyond the soccer fields.

Julia eyed him curiously as Nicola bent down to get something from her soccer bag. I could tell she was listening. "Why do you think he's a scout?" Julia asked.

"I don't recognize him. He's not one of the parents," I answered.

"So? He could be a parent on the other team."

"None of the parents dress like that."

"They do if they just came from work," argued Julia.

"At ten o'clock on a Saturday morning?" I scoffed. "Get real."

"Some people work weekends. Realtors, for instance," Julia said.

"You're only saying that because your mom is one. And he has a clipboard. Look, he's taking notes."

Finally, Julia paid attention. "Well, I suppose he could be...but he seems to be paying more attention to the scenery than the game."

The coach motioned to us. "Get ready to go back on, girls. Last shift before half-time."

I stood up. "This time," I said, "I'm going to score."

Julia grinned. "Not if I get the ball first." And she raced me out onto the field.

chapter two

"See you later, Dad!" I called. I slammed the minivan door. Julia and Nicola hopped out the other side and the three of us raced across the field toward the practice field. It was Monday after school, our first practice since the last game.

A couple of other girls from the team were already there, standing around.

"What's going on?" I asked.

Kaitlin looked at me, her eyebrows arched. "Have a look," she said. I glanced in the direction she pointed.

The goalposts looked totally normal at first. But then I could see that the nets had been slashed—the nylon mesh hung in tattered fragments like a hula skirt.

"What happened?" Julia asked.

Kaitlin shrugged. "No idea. We just got here, and it was like that."

I walked over to have a look. The mesh was heavy, strong nylon cord, and it had been deliberately cut with scissors or cutters—the cord wasn't frayed the way it would have been if someone had sawed at it with a knife.

Julia joined me. "Someone came prepared to do this," I whispered. "It wasn't just random vandalism."

"What do you mean?" Julia asked. I explained to her why I thought it had been deliberate.

"Why would anybody want to do that?" Julia wanted to know.

"I don't know." I felt uneasy. Something about this didn't feel right. I'd seen vandalism before, of course: spray-painted graffiti on the school's walls, handwritten messages inside toilet cubicles. Even the thick glass had been smashed at the bus shelter on my street. All of those things were aimed at sending a message of rebellion to the world. This was different. This was a deliberate strike against our team—against all the soccer teams that used the field. Why?

A figure in a dark tracksuit hefted a bright yellow mesh bag of soccer balls over his shoulder and started across the field toward us. It was Dan Collins, our coach.

"What's the matter?" Coach asked, dropping the balls on the grass. "Why aren't you girls warming up?"

I gestured to the nets. "The park had a visitor," I said.

Coach looked disgusted. "Some kids just have nothing better to do," he said. "Come on, let's get started." He emptied the balls out onto the grass. "Each of you grab one, and we'll start by doing some laps around the field, dribbling the ball."

Before we had completed even one lap,

a truck with the city parks logo on the door pulled onto the grass near the edge of the field.

"You can't practice here today," a woman called, striding across the grass.

Coach crossed his arms over his chest. "Why not?" he asked, frowning. Coach took practices very seriously and insisted we did too. Canceling wasn't really an option.

"We've just had a case of vandalism reported. No one can use the field until we've investigated," explained the young woman.

"There's nothing to investigate," Coach snorted. "Some kids with too much time on their hands decided to make trouble. Why should that interrupt our practice?"

"Because we haven't had a chance to make sure the field is safe," the young woman said. "How do you know that the vandals haven't smashed beer bottles somewhere in the grass? One of your players could get hurt. I'm sorry, but the field is closed until further notice."

"But this is our assigned field," Coach sputtered. "Where is my team supposed to practice?"

"You'll have to take that up with your soccer association," the young woman said firmly. "But for now, I'll have to ask you and your players to leave."

I began to gather up the soccer balls and put them back inside the mesh bag. Coach looked as though he wanted to argue, but then he shrugged.

"Come on, girls. I guess we'll have to get hold of your parents. Practice is cancelled."

chapter three

"That was just weird," Julia said at school the next day.

"What was?" I stashed my math book in my locker and grabbed my science text, adding it to the massive pile of binders and notebooks in my arms. I blew a stray curl out of my eyes and wished I had another hand to straighten my glasses, which were sitting crooked on my nose. I only have to wear them for school, and I think they're a giant pain. Plus they make my eyes look bigger—which would be okay if they were a gorgeous blue like Julia's, but they're not. They're a muddy hazel. Not exactly my choice of color.

"That someone would wreck our soccer nets." Julia glanced at me. "Do you really need all that stuff? You look like a walking book tower."

"Half of it is Nicola's. I'm giving it back to her. The custodian needed to fix her locker door, so she had to move her books out for a day. And I have a science test after lunch. I'm going to study after we eat."

As we walked down the crowded hallway, the books grew heavier. "Do you see her anywhere?" I asked. I hoisted the books higher.

"Not yet."

"Let's hurry up. These things are killing my arms." I shoved one of the doors at the end of the hall open with my hip, turned quickly to go through it and hit someone coming from the other direction with the impact of a Mack truck.

"Hey!" he yelled. The next thing I knew, half of my books had slipped from my grasp and something slimy was dripping down my arm.

"Aggh!" I screeched. I threw the remaining books up in the air. Papers and notebooks rained down like confetti and scattered all over the floor. I shook my arm frantically as big gobs of yellowish goo slid off my skin and landed with a squishy noise on the notebooks. "Oh, gross! What *is* that?" I yelped.

"That," said Drew Collins, holding a cardboard tray full of plastic containers, which were now tipped and leaking, "is what's left of my science project."

Drew Collins. My face grew hot. I wanted to die. I've liked Drew for ages, but he'd never noticed me before. This wasn't exactly what I had mind, though.

"I'm really sorry," I croaked. My cheeks felt as though they would burst into flames.

Drew sighed and put down the tray. "Here. Let me help you pick up this mess."

I shook a final blob off my arm. "Is this stuff, uh...dangerous?"

"No, my project was on viscosity. That was just gelatin dissolved in colored water."

"Oh." Brilliant remark, I thought. "Are you interested in science?" Even better, I said to myself. Why not comment on the weather?

"Sort of. Right now I'm just interested in passing." Drew finished stacking all the loose sheets of paper and handed them to me.

"Yeah, me too. I have a huge test this afternoon."

Drew picked up his tray. "Well, good luck. See you around."

"See you." I gave him a feeble smile, and then I immediately wanted to kick myself. How could I have been so stupid as to smash into the cutest guy in the whole school and destroy his entire science project?

"You okay?" Julia said. I'd forgotten she was even there.

"Yeah. Terminally embarrassed but basically fine." I shook my head in dismay.

"Well, I think you finally got his attention. There's no way he'll forget you now." Julia grinned.

"Shut up!" I squeaked. "I just had the most humiliating experience of my life. The least you could do is be sympathetic!" All the girls liked Drew, and it wasn't just because he was athletic and had thick brown hair, warm brown eyes and the greatest smile. He was funny and nice, and I wished I'd found a different way to finally talk to him.

"Come on, let's find Nicola so you can unload that pile of books. I'll help you carry them." Julia was just reaching for several when her phone went off. "Hang on, Iz. My mom said she might call at lunch today." But as Julia flipped open her cell phone, her whole face changed. Her smile shrank to a small tight frown, and her eyes narrowed.

"What's wrong?" I asked.

Julia held out the phone. "Look," she said.

A text message scrolled across the tiny screen:

LOSE THE GAME OR U

WILL B CRBT SOCCER QUEEN.

"What?" I said. "What does that mean?"

Julia looked up at me uneasily. "Lose the game, or you will be crying really big tears, soccer queen," she said.

"That's awful." I felt my anger rise.

"I guess they must mean the next soccer game," Julia said. "Someone must be worried about the regional tournament."

I peered at the message. "Who's it from?"

Julia pressed a button on the phone, and then she shook her head. "I don't know. The sender is blocked." She shrugged and deleted the message.

"Wait!" I cried. "That was evidence!"

"Evidence of what?" Julia said.

"Of making threats, or bullying, or whatever you want to call it," I answered.

"They can threaten all they want," replied Julia. "I'll still play the way I always do."

"You have to tell the coach about this," I said.

"What for? Coach can't do anything. We have no idea who sent it." Julia pocketed the cell phone and held open the hall door for me. "Come on, let's go eat."

"Julia..."

"Somebody's just fooling around, Iz. Forget it."

But I couldn't. As I followed Julia with my messy stack of books, I was sure there was more to that message than some dumb joke.

chapter four

I hoisted my soccer bag over my shoulder and traipsed over the field, the rain-wet grass swishing against my cleats. I shivered. My socks were already damp, and the thick gray clouds overhead looked as though they were ready to dump another load of rain. The wind blew in cold gusts. I could tell this was going to be a wonderful practice. There are definitely times when I wish I'd taken up a nice, warm indoor sport—like Ping-Pong, for instance.

The coach had his back to me as I marched grimly up to the sidelines. He was talking to someone. I paid no attention as I dumped my bag on the grass and fished a practice ball out of the mesh bag nearby. I was about to go out on the field to warm up, when Coach turned around.

"Hi, Isabella," he said. Then I realized who was with him. I wished the earth would swallow me whole.

"Hi, Drew," I said weakly. "What are you doing here?"

"I came to help my dad out with practice," he said.

His dad? I thought. Then I realized—Drew Collins, Dan Collins—I just never connected the two.

"You guys know each other?" asked Coach.

"We've run into each other at school." Drew grinned. "Right, Izzy?" That grin made me feel a whole lot better.

"Well, once anyway," I said.

The coach wasn't listening. "What's going on over there?" He pointed across the field to the wooded area of the park. After the vandalized nets had been cleared away, we were allowed to practice on the field again, but now a number of city workers were posting small yellow signs around the copse of trees. Some areas were being blocked off with yellow tape.

Julia, Nicola and a bunch of others hurried across the grass from the parking lot.

"Sorry we're late, Coach," Julia puffed. She dropped her soccer gear and her overstuffed backpack on the ground. "My mom had to stop for gas."

Coach was still watching the city workers. "It's all right, girls. Get a ball. Let's start warming up."

Julia glanced at me in surprise. Coach is usually very strict about us being on time for practice, but it was obvious he was distracted by the beehive of activity going on at the far side of the park. He didn't even look surprised when, a few minutes later, one of the workers approached us on the field.

"Excuse me, sir. Are you the coach of this team?" he said.

"Yes," Coach answered warily.

"I'll have to ask you and your team to leave."

I thought Coach Collins was about to explode. His face turned a mottled purple and the veins bulged in his temples. I could see him weighing his words. I held my breath.

"My team was instructed to leave this field last week, when our nets were vandalized. I was told that it was a safety procedure. Why are we being asked to leave now?" Coach's voice was controlled.

"The city has received a complaint about possible chemical contamination at this site. It's important that no one use this recreational area until that contamination is confirmed."

"What's involved in that?" asked Coach Collins.

"Soil samples, different types of testing," the worker said.

"So how long are we looking at?" Coach frowned.

"Don't know. Indefinitely." The worker gestured toward the woods. "There's quite a lot of area."

Coach Collins threw his hands up. "This is unbelievable! My team has nowhere to practice. We have a regional tournament coming up!"

"Sorry, sir. That's not my problem."

"Look, we've practiced on this field for three years now," Coach argued. "There's never been a problem before. Why now?"

"We're not certain," the worker said. "But it is important that you and the kids leave the area immediately and find somewhere else to practice until this park is proven to be safe." With that, he turned and strode back to his colleagues, leaving Coach staring after him.

"Come on, girls," Coach said wearily. "I guess we have to go. At this rate we'll be practicing for the championship in my basement!"

chapter five

Sweat dripped down my face as I ran. My hair, which I had tied back and corkscrewed into a tight knot at the back of my head, was slowly coming loose. Strands stuck to my damp forehead, but I had no time to push them away. I kept my eyes on the ball every second.

"Izzy, get back!" Coach shouted from the sidelines. I glanced over to see an opposing player trying to get open farther down the field. I moved to cover her as the player with the ball broke away and sent a pass in our direction.

I dug hard with my cleats, fighting for the ball. It turned into a bit of a private wrestling match—I took an elbow in the ribs that the ref didn't see—but I didn't give up. I punched the ball out with my foot. Julia appeared from nowhere and took the ball up the field.

The players from the other team shot after her, but I lagged behind. Playing defense today gave me an opportunity to hang back, and I really needed it. This team was way too good and was pushing us very hard.

They were passing all around us, forcing us to run for the ball to get possession. I already felt like I'd run miles. My throat was so dry, it almost hurt to breathe. All I was waiting for at this point was Coach's signal to come off. I wondered what was taking him so long.

Then I heard the cheering from the bench, and I knew why. Julia still had possession, and Coach wasn't pulling her off while she had a chance to score. I watched her dodge through the other team's players, saw Nicola move up to support her. Julia passed, Nicola took the shot and Julia dove in for the rebound. Like she had done so many times with me, she fired on the net while the goalie was still gathering herself from Nicola's onslaught. The ball sailed through the posts and buried itself in the top corner.

Another goal, and this time a badly needed one.

Coach called for the switch. Julia and I ran off with Nicola close behind. Nicola's face looked puckery and pinched, like she'd swallowed a lemon. I could tell she was fighting the same annoyance I felt every time Julia captured a spectacular goal after I set her up. The difference was, Julia and I could joke about it. While I kept telling myself that soccer is a team sport, and any goal is good for the team, I wasn't so sure Nicola felt the same way.

Julia rummaged in her soccer bag for her water bottle and came up with her cell phone in one hand.

I chugged a drink from my own bottle. "What's the matter?"

"Oh, it went off before the game, but I didn't have time to check it." Julia took a sip of water and flipped the phone open. She pressed a few buttons, then her eyes widened. "Izzy, look!" she whispered.

I glanced at the tiny screen.

LOSER! U SUCK JULIA.

"That came in just before the game," Julia said. "But look at this one." She pressed another button, and a second message flashed up.

REMMBR, LOSE OR ELSE.
I CAN MAKE U VERY SORRY.

Julia looked shaken. "What do they mean? Do you think someone would hurt me?"

"Punch you out in the parking lot after the game, you mean?" Suddenly I was furious. "No, not with all of us there. But if it's someone on the other team, they might try something out on the field." I looked Julia straight in the eye. "You have to tell the coach. He needs to know what's going on."

"Iz, we're in the middle of the game! He can't focus on this right now."

I rubbed my forehead and tried to think of a solution. "We need someone who can watch what's going on during the game, especially while you're on the field. I'm on the same shift with you, so I can't." I scanned the crowd of parents. My eyes landed briefly on Drew, who had obviously been dragged to the game by his dad. He was sitting just behind us, and he had headphones in his ears, a textbook in his lap and a portable game player in his hands. He wasn't even watching the game.

"What about Drew?" I whispered. "He could watch, see if anything suspicious is going on."

"Okay." Julia handed the phone to me. "You ask him."

"Me? Why me?" I stalled.

"Because you like him. And you talked to him."

"I dumped a slimy science project on him, you mean," I said. I felt my face flush just thinking about it.

"So what? I don't even know the guy. Go." Julia gave me a gentle push in Drew's direction.

I looked back with pleading eyes.

"Go on!" Julia said. "And hurry up. We're about to switch again."

I walked over to Drew. "Hi," I said nervously.

"Hey!" Drew smiled and plucked the headphones from his ears. "Great game."

"You weren't even watching!" I couldn't help grinning.

"I watched while you were on," Drew said.

The implication of that made me forget for a second what I was there for. I willed myself not to blush. Then I saw Julia motioning frantically, and knew I didn't have much time before I had to get back on the field.

"Listen, Drew. I need your help," I said. "My friend Julia has been getting some really mean text messages on her cell phone." I showed him the most recent one on the phone. "We think someone is trying to scare her into throwing the game. Can you keep an eye out for anyone who looks like they are up to something?"

"Wow. Sure. I'll watch. Which one is Julia?"

"The one making faces over there." I pointed to Julia, who was still making exaggerated gestures for me to get my butt back over there.

"Okay. Good luck!" Drew said.

"Thanks!" I called back. I ran out onto the field with the rest of my shift. Julia shot me a questioning glance, and I gave her a quick thumbs-up. She nodded and took her position.

We were down to the last few minutes of the game. The other team played hard but showed no signs of being overly rough or threatening. No one targeted Julia at all.

When the whistle blew to end the game, Julia joined me, breathless. We shook hands with the other team, and then we hurried to the sidelines, where Drew was waiting.

"Well?" I said.

Drew shook his head. "Nothing."

Julia sighed. "I wish we knew who it was. The first message didn't seem like a big deal, but if this keeps going on..." She let her voice trail off.

"We'll figure it out," I encouraged her. "Don't worry."

"I know." Julia bent down to pick up her soccer bag. She paused, and then she looked inside.

"What's wrong?" I asked.

"My extra shin guards are gone! And there's a big hole in the bottom of the bag." Her face had gone white. "It looks like someone slashed it with a knife!"

chapter six

"Listen, Drew," I said urgently. "Did you notice anyone fooling around with Julia's bag during the game? Anyone at all?"

Drew shook his head. "Nope. But then, I wasn't watching the bags. I was watching you and Julia and the other team. The bags were all piled up together. Your team was always going through them to get water bottles and extra stuff."

"So, as far as you could tell, no one who wasn't on the team could have gotten to the bag during the game?"

"What is this, a police interrogation? No, I don't think so, but I can't be sure."

I turned to Julia. "Did you notice if your shin guards were in the bag or whether that hole was there before the game?

Julia chewed her lip. "I don't know...my jacket was stuffed in the bottom. The hole could have been there. My extra shin guards were in the bag at practice last night. I can't remember seeing them before the game..."

"So someone could have vandalized your soccer bag anytime, not necessarily during the game," I speculated. I bent down to have a closer look at the bag. It was made of heavy nylon, and the rip was clean—there were no ragged edges that might indicate that the fabric had been torn. I had to agree. It looked like it had been done with a knife. That also meant that it might not have been obvious. Someone could have reached inside with a small box cutter and sliced the hole without anyone realizing what was going on.

"Weird. Why are they targeting you?" Drew asked Julia.

Julia hesitated.

"Because she's the best player on the team," I answered. "We thought maybe someone wanted to scare her into losing the game for our team, to make their chances of getting to the Regionals better. But now I'm not so sure."

"What do you mean?" Julia asked.

"Well, our soccer nets were cut to shreds. Now there's some bogus complaint about chemical contamination at our field, and we have no place to practice."

"How do you know it's bogus?" said Drew.

"I don't. But why would there suddenly be a problem with the field? We've been playing there ever since the community built it." I shook my head. "It doesn't make sense."

"It does if someone just found evidence of chemicals," Julia argued.

"But why now? Why when you've also gotten threats and the nets have also been damaged? It seems like a pretty big coincidence. I think someone is targeting the whole team!" I said.

"I don't know about this, Iz," Julia whispered nervously. She drew the hood of her sweatshirt over her head and tucked her nose down inside. "If this chemical thing is legit, don't you think it's kind of dangerous to be here?"

"No more than when we were practicing out here and didn't know anything about it. We've been breathing this air for months!" I answered. I ducked under the yellow tape that surrounded the wooded area.

"Oh, that makes me feel a lot better," Julia said. "We could have been breathing poisonous gas for all you know."

"Well, none of us is dead yet, so I think we're probably okay to go check this out. If there are any clues to find, this is where they'll be."

The grass felt cool with the shady damp of a late spring evening. The mosquitoes rose in swarms over the field, but I had sprayed us with enough bug repellant that they stayed away. Darkened trees fluttered their leaves in the wind. The place would have been peaceful, if Julia and I weren't so tense about getting caught. If someone was targeting our soccer team, they might be a little hostile if they found us.

"Come on. This is dumb," I hissed. "We won't find anything by standing here."

But Julia didn't move. She swallowed hard and pointed with a trembling finger toward the copse of trees nearest us. A dark hooded figure was moving slowly through the shadows toward us.

I stifled a scream as the person emerged and lunged toward us. My heart froze. My feet refused to move. Horrified, I waited for the worst.

Instead, I watched in amazement as the figure's lunge didn't end with grabbing me in a strangle hold, but finished with a huge face-plant into the earth.

"Darn tree roots!" a familiar voice cursed.

"Drew?" I shrieked.

He lifted his mud-streaked face. "Yeah?" he answered sheepishly. He pushed the hood on his sweatshirt back.

"What are you doing here?" Relief sent a tingling shock through my whole body.

Drew stood up and brushed the dead leaves from his jeans. "Same thing you guys are, probably. My dad thinks something strange is going on, so I decided to check things out."

"Find anything?" I said.

Drew shook his head. "Not yet."

I glanced at the rapidly darkening sky. "We'd better hurry. There's not much light left to see any clues." I tugged Julia along.

"I don't even know what we're looking for," she complained.

"Anything. Something that might give a hint to why somebody wants to make trouble for our team," I answered. I began searching the ground. After ten minutes, I'd found a few remnants of yellow tape, a lost pen and a few discarded pop cans, but that was it. Drew was deep in the aspen grove, and Julia was looking along the perimeter of the soccer field.

I plopped down on a park bench, which sat just at the edge of the natural area, overlooking the sports fields. Think, I told myself. There has to be a clue somewhere. Absently, I ran my finger over the engraved plaque in the center of the bench. The plaque read:

Because her family farmed this land for generations, it was the last wish of Denise Ausby that this original homestead be given to the city as a recreational area for all to enjoy.

Nice, I thought. Some old lady gave us this land so we could all play on it, and now it's off limits.

"Hey, Izzy!" Drew called. "I found something!"

I bolted up off the bench. "What is it?" I hurried over.

"It's some kind of form. I think it might have to do with the testing," said Drew. Julia came running across the field.

I took the paper from him and examined it. The form was blank, but on the other side, scribbled handwriting was visible. It was smudged and hard to read—some words were abbreviated, but the one thing I could clearly read was the word "negative."

"It's someone's notes from whoever was out here testing for chemicals," I said. "*And it looks like they didn't find any!*"

chapter seven

"City Hall." The voice on the other end of the phone sounded bored.

"Hi. I'd like to speak to someone in charge of the city parks, please," I said.

"I'll transfer you."

I waited while elevator music played. There was a clatter as someone finally picked up the receiver.

"Bob Greene here."

"Mr. Greene, my name is Isabella MacAllister. I'd like to ask you a few questions about the recreational area that's been closed in Briarwood."

"Yes?" He sounded wary.

"I'd like to know why it's been closed."

"We've received a complaint regarding possible soil contamination, and it's our procedure to close a public area until we can investigate."

"I know that. I meant, more specifically," I said.

"I'm afraid I can't release specific details."

"I live in that neighborhood. I play soccer on that field. If there's something going on that could affect my health, I have a right to know about it."

"How old are you?" Mr. Greene demanded.

"Fourteen. What does that have to do with anything?"

"I don't have to explain myself to a kid."

"Well, then you can start explaining to the media, because that will be my next call."

There was silence on the other end of the line.

"You're pretty gutsy," he said finally. "Okay, what do you want to know?"

"I want to know what the contamination is, and I want to know why this is suddenly a problem three years after the park was built."

"The concern is about several different kinds of contamination. Solvents and pesticides are possibilities, but the main concern is lead. Lead can cause all kinds of health issues, especially in kids. I received a phone call from a fellow who said he is a descendant of the Ausby family who owned the land. He told me that his grandfather used to do quite a bit of carpentry work in one of the barns to make some extra money to help run the farm. As a result, a lot of paint was disposed of in a homemade landfill on the land. Then there was a big fire that leveled the original homestead and the carpentry shop along with it around 1970. This guy is concerned that the level of lead created from dumping lead-based paints is significant enough to warrant us looking into it."

"Why now?"

"I don't know. It would have saved us a lot of trouble and money if we had cleaned up the soil when the park was built. The guy said that—told me he feels responsible since the property belonged to his family. He offered to buy the land back and get it cleaned up himself, but I told him that wasn't necessary."

"Have you found any evidence yet?" I tried not to sound too eager.

"Well, we've found some lead contamination, but not near the home site. It's scattered in concentrated spots some distance away. I can't say for sure that there's enough of a concern to close the park permanently, but we should have some more answers in another week or two."

"Thank you, Mr. Greene. I really appreciate you telling me this."

"Good. Now let me get back to work." He hung up.

I stared at the phone absently. If this guy

who made the complaint was concerned about kids getting sick from lead contamination, then it didn't sound like there was a connection between that, the vandalized soccer nets and Julia's threatening messages.

I chewed on the end of a pencil. I'd been so sure the incidents were linked. Now I'd hit a dead end, and I didn't know what to do next.

chapter eight

LOSERLOSERLOSERLOSER
LOSERLOSERLOSERLOSER
LOSERLOSERLOSERLOSER

"They aren't very original, are they?" I commented.

Julia hit the delete button with a vicious click and threw the cell phone into her soccer bag. "I'm getting really sick of this.

Who's *doing* it?" She glared at the other team, warming up at the other end of the field.

"I don't know, Jules. Could be anybody." I sighed. I stretched out on the grass and began some sit-ups. This was an away game, which was great, since we still didn't have a replacement field for our team yet.

"I'd like to know how they got my cell phone number, for starters," Julia grumbled. She flopped down beside me and started stretching her leg muscles.

I sat bolt upright. Of course! Why hadn't I thought of that before? Julia's cell phone was unlisted. Whoever had been threatening Julia had to have access to our team phone list.

"Julia, that's it!" I cried. "It's someone who's got our team phone numbers!"

"Yeah, that really narrows it down," Julia said sarcastically. "A copy of that list could have been left anywhere."

"Maybe, but it's still a clue," I countered. "We could ask around and see if someone lost their list."

"What good would that do? We'd still be no farther ahead in finding out who this person is. What we need," Julia said with determination, "is a hacker. I'm sure there must be some way to get into computer records and find out where text messages are being sent from. I just don't know how to do it."

"Me neither," I said. I went back to doing sit-ups, but after a few, I stopped again. "What we need is a list of suspects. People we think might be likely to want us out of the Regionals."

"That would be pretty much every team we play," said Julia. "We've won the Regionals for the last three years.

I frowned at her. "We have to start somewhere."

"I know." Julia rubbed her forehead in exasperation. "I'm just mad, that's all. I hate it that someone can make me feel this way."

"Don't. Don't let them," I said, giving her shoulder a quick squeeze. "That's what they're trying to do."

Julia just nodded.

"Come on, girls!" Coach motioned for us to get out on the field. "Let's do a few practice shots to warm up the goalie before the game starts."

I jumped up, but I couldn't get my mind off the threats. Who in particular might want Julia to play badly? But even though I thought carefully through all of the players I knew from other teams, no one seemed to have a really clear motive. All of them wanted to win, of course. But no one stood out as a strong suspect. I had to agree with Julia—the list from that angle was too long.

We were missing a clue. I knew it. But I didn't know where to find it.

"Izzy, pass back!"

I could hear Coach shouting frantically from the sidelines. I was hemmed in on all sides by players from the opposing team. There was no way I could get a pass through them. The pressure was definitely on. With a quick move, I followed Coach's advice. I tried to give the ball a deft kick backward to Nicola, but I overshot the mark. I winced as Nicola had to scramble to get it.

Glaring at me, she dribbled it sideways, dodging the players who had been covering me. She raced for the net, but I saw her hesitate when she noticed Julia hovering near the goal. Julia was trying to evade the defensive player who was marking her and still stay clear for a pass.

Nicola frowned and tried to make a more careful approach to the net by deking the goalie out with some fancy footwork, but it didn't work. One of the defensemen swiped the ball and passed it down the field before Nicola could even fight for possession.

The ref blew the whistle. Coach motioned us off the field for the switch.

"Why didn't you take the shot?" Julia was clearly frustrated with Nicola.

"Because you were up at the net, cherry-picking, as usual," Nicola answered hotly. "I'm getting tired of you always scooping the rebound and taking credit for the goal."

"Then get the ball in the net the first time!" Julia snapped.

Nicola's cheeks turned red. She opened her mouth to retort, but Julia cut her off.

"And I'm not cherry-picking. Last time I checked, soccer was a team sport. That means any goal is good, no matter who scores," said Julia.

"Yeah. Whatever." Nicola turned away, grabbed her water bottle and sat down with some of the other girls on our team.

"What's her problem?" Julia asked, shaking her head.

"I don't know," I answered. "Maybe she's just a little uptight. That business guy is here with the clipboard again."

"Really? Where?" Julia craned her neck to see where I was pointing.

"Over there. And he's with your mom!"

"What?" Julia tried to keep the excitement off her face, but I could tell what she was thinking. If that guy really was a scout, and he was talking to her mother, it could mean only one thing. He was interested in getting Julia on the national team for our age group.

The whistle blew to end the game, and Julia could hardly contain herself until we'd shaken hands with the other team and grabbed our soccer bags. She hurried over to her mother, with me close behind.

"Great game, honey!" Mrs. Hintz hugged Julia. "You were terrific too, Isabella."

"Thanks, Mrs. Hintz," I said.

"Isabella, do you think your parents would mind dropping Julia off at home? I had to arrange to meet a client here. It's a fairly urgent matter, and he couldn't wait. I'm going to take him back to the office to fill out some paperwork, and it would help if I could go right away."

"Sure, Mrs. Hintz. I'm sure that would be okay."

"That guy's a client?" Julia said, disappointment evident in her voice.

"Yes, his name's Richard Ausby. He's interested in buying some land that belongs to the city. Something like that is quite an involved process, so I need to go through a bunch of forms with him."

Something about that name seemed familiar.

"Why?" Julia was pouting.

"Because the land's not for sale yet, so the offer is a little more complicated," said Mrs. Hintz, with a touch of exasperation. "He's demanding the offer be prepared right away. I'm sorry, Julia. I don't like this anymore than you do."

Julia was no longer listening. "It's okay. See you at home, Mom." She steered me toward my own parents, who were talking with Coach. "He wasn't a scout at all," she hissed, pulling me to a stop. "Whose dumb idea was that, anyway?"

"Yours, I think," I said.

"I'm almost positive it was your idea," said Julia.

"Well, maybe," I admitted.

"So I'm not listening to you anymore."

"Fine," I agreed. We started walking toward Coach again. I looked down. "Uh, Julia?"

"I'm not listening."

"Yeah, but..."

"I'm still not listening."

"But your shoelace..." I was interrupted by Julia stepping on it and falling flat on her face. "...is undone."

chapter nine

"Hey, Izzy," Drew came up behind me in the line at the cafeteria. "Want to sit together for lunch?"

My face tingled. I was sure I was blushing. "Sure."

"Heard it was a great game on Saturday."

"Not bad." I glanced up at him. "But I have a really bad habit of falling apart just when I need to score. I'm scared your dad is going to bench me if I can't get it together."

Drew shook his head. "He won't. You're a great player, Iz. You just need to believe that you can do it. I know it's hard when the other team is coming right at you."

"No kidding! It doesn't help when you know you're going to have to face your own team after the game, either. Sometimes they don't make it easy. You should've heard Julia and Nicola fighting at the last game." I glanced over my shoulder, where Nicola was seated with some friends at a table nearby.

"What do you mean?" asked Drew.

I filled him in on the argument between Nicola and Julia. Drew just shrugged.

"It's always like that on competitive teams. Someone's always trying to outdo everyone else," he said.

"I guess so," I said doubtfully.

"Besides, Julia is kind of a ball hog. I can see why Nicola would get mad." Drew reached ahead of me for a plastic fork from the bin.

"What!" I raised my eyebrows. "Julia's my best friend."

"So?" Drew snorted. "That doesn't change the way she plays soccer."

"And how is that, exactly?" I said ominously.

Drew didn't get the hint. "Well, she showboats. She's out there for number one, that's for sure. She never passes when she thinks she can take the shot."

"Well, why should she?" I said heatedly. "The object of the game is to score, you know. And since when are you such an expert on soccer?"

Drew looked a little taken aback, but he frowned. "I play. And my dad coaches. So I think I know what I'm talking about," he retorted.

"I wouldn't be so sure about that," I said.

"Look, Iz. Soccer's a team sport. Everyone should play to help the team, not themselves."

"Julia doesn't!" I hissed, aware that people were beginning to stare. "Scoring helps the team win, if you haven't figured that out yet!"

Drew slammed his tray down. "I don't know what you're getting so mad about, but you can eat lunch by yourself. I'll go sit with the guys." He glared at me. "See you around, Iz."

"Not if I see you first!" I fired back. He stomped away. I turned back to the front of the line and reached for the first drink I saw. It was veggie blend, which I hate, but I didn't care. I threw it on my tray along with my brown-bagged lunch, paid the cashier and found a seat. What had made me say those things to Drew, anyway?

I opened my lunch bag with trembling hands. My plastic-wrapped sandwich, carrot sticks and veggie drink had about the same appeal as a bowl of mud with chocolate sauce. I looked down at the table and willed myself not to cry. Not here, in front of everybody. But a tear ran down my nose and splashed on my sandwich.

"Hey, what's going on?" Julia sat down beside me.

"Nothing," I muttered. "Where were you?"

"I got called to the office just before the bell. My mom had to drop off my social studies assignment. I forgot it at home." Julia lowered her voice. "What's wrong?"

"Drew just humiliated me in front of the whole lunch room, that's all," I said, my voice breaking.

"He did?" Julia looked instantly incensed. "That jerk! Why? What did he say?"

I had to laugh, even though I felt horrible. Julia was so ready to defend me, even without knowing what had happened. Then I realized I had done the same for her. True idiots, but true friends, I suppose.

"Well, actually it was about you. First he asked me to sit with him at lunch, and then he criticized the way you play soccer and I got mad, so I told him off. He slammed his tray down and told me to forget about eating lunch together and left."

"Why were you guys even talking about me?" asked Julia.

"I told him what happened with Nicola."

"Oh." Julia took a bite of her sandwich. "And I suppose he said something about Nicola having a right to be mad."

I stared at her in amazement. "How did you know?"

"Because apparently Nicola complained to the coach, so Coach talked to me about it. He said that he could see how Nicola might feel that way, and he told me to make sure that I pass the ball off if I'm not in the clear, but he also told me to keep on scoring. Maybe Drew heard Coach talking about it at home or something and didn't get all the details."

I felt worse. I glanced across the lunchroom, but Drew's back was to me. He was joking around with some of the other guys and seemed to be having a good time. I stiffened. Nicola was walking up to him. I could see her flash him a bright smile, and she stopped to talk.

Julia followed my gaze. "What's she up to now?" she asked.

"I don't know," I answered grimly. "But I don't like it at all."

chapter ten

I glanced up to make sure my social studies teacher and the librarian were still deep in conversation, and then I clicked off the report I'd been working on. The computer hummed. Quickly, I logged onto the Internet. I typed "Richard Ausby" into the search engine and waited.

Something about that name bothered me. There was more going on than Julia's mom selling this guy some land. I just knew it.

Results came up for some Richard Ausby in Milton, California. I knew that wasn't what I was looking for, so I scrolled down until I reached Denise Ausby's obituary. It gave Richard Ausby as one of the family members' names, and told of Denise's gift to her community by turning her land over to the public for recreational use. Remembering the plaque on the bench at the park, I selected the entry. Someone stopped near my cubicle.

I looked up. It was Drew.

I looked down again quickly, my shoulders tight. I could feel him watching me, but after a moment he began to look for a book at the opposite end of the aisle.

The tension hung in the air. Neither of us said a word.

Within a few minutes Drew found the book he was looking for and left. I turned my attention back to the computer's search results. The obituary didn't give any information about Richard Ausby, so I clicked onto the next site on the list.

To my surprise, I saw a heading about the last train robbery in Canada.

On August 2, 1920, local miners George Arkoff, Richard Ausby and Tom Bassoff robbed Canadian Pacific Railway's train No. 63 at gunpoint, hoping to find several well-known wealthy rumrunners aboard. After stripping passengers of their money and jewelry, including a priceless ruby necklace, the men escaped. Eluding the Royal Canadian Mounted Police and the CPR Police, Ausby escaped into the United States with the bulk of the loot while Bassoff and Arkoff remained in the area. On August 7, the two were spotted in a local café. Three constables entered the café through the front and back doors, and in the ensuing shootout, Arkoff, an RCMP constable and an Alberta Provincial Police constable were killed, while Bassoff, though wounded, escaped into the rubble of the Frank Slide. Bassoff was eventually apprehended without incident on August 11 at Pincher Station, thirty-five kilometers to the east.

Although testimony suggests that the police officers had failed to identify themselves and had probably fired first, Bassoff was found guilty of murder and hanged in Lethbridge, Alberta, on December 22, 1920.

Richard Ausby was captured in 1924 near Butte, Montana, after trying to sell a distinctive railway watch. Ausby, who had not been involved in the shootout, was returned to Alberta where he was sentenced to seven years imprisonment. He died in prison in 1926 without revealing where the rest of the stolen goods were hidden. The remainder of the loot, including the ruby necklace, was never found.

I looked up with a gasp. This couldn't be the same Richard Ausby who had been at our soccer games. But Ausby wasn't a very common name. Could the Richard Ausby from 1920 be a relative? And more importantly, could the stolen loot have something to do with why our park was closed down? I printed out the article and picked it up.

I needed to talk to Julia and Drew. But since I wasn't speaking to Drew right now, and Julia was in gym class, that was difficult. I stood there for a minute, burning with indecision and humiliation. Then I swallowed my pride and went to find Drew. He was sitting at a computer station across the library.

"Drew?" I whispered.

"What?" He didn't look at me.

"I need to talk to you."

"So, talk." He wasn't making this easy.

"Look, I'm sorry I got so mad at you. But Julia's my friend. I don't like hearing her criticized," I said.

"I wasn't trying to criticize her," Drew said. "I just overheard my dad—"

"And then," I broke in, the words just bursting out, "you were all buddy-buddy with Nicola right after we got into that fight."

Drew stared at me. "I was being polite."

"Could have fooled me," I said bitterly.

"Look, she asked if I wanted to go to the movies with her. I said no. End of story," said Drew. "There's only one girl I'm interested in going to the movies with right now, but I have to say she's acting pretty weird."

"Are you talking about me?" I demanded.

"Do I really have to spell it out for you, Izzy?" Drew's gaze was steady.

"Well..." I swallowed, unsure of how to react. Part of me was thrilled. *He liked me*! The other part was embarrassed that I'd gotten so mad for nothing. "I'm sorry I made such a big deal out of everything." I hesitated. "Okay?"

"Okay." Drew reached out and gave my hand a quick squeeze, crumpling the computer printout that I still held. "I didn't mean to make you mad."

I glanced down at the papers in my hand. "Drew, there's something else I need to tell you." I pushed my printout toward him. "Have a look at this."

Drew saved his document on the computer, picked up the printout and began to read. "Yeah, so?" he said when he'd finished.

I worked hard to suppress my irritation. "Doesn't the name Ausby mean anything to you?"

"Nope, not really," Drew shrugged.

"Are you sure?"

"Why, Iz? How is a train robbery that happened almost ninety years ago important?"

"Ausby's the name on the park bench at the edge of the woods by the soccer field, the one that dedicates the family's land to the city."

Drew frowned in thought. "It could be. I didn't look that closely. Do you want to tell me what's going on?"

"Julia's mom met with a guy after the game on Saturday—a guy named Richard Ausby. He's interested in buying some land from the city—land that isn't for sale yet. How much do you want to bet he's bidding on the Ausby land that our soccer field was built on?"

"Maybe." Drew looked doubtful. "But why?"

"Good question. I don't know. But I'm almost positive it has something to do with this train robbery."

Drew scanned the paragraphs again. "It says here that the rest of the loot was never found. Maybe the first Richard Ausby brought it to that homestead and hid it there. The Crowsnest Pass is only about two hours away from Calgary by car. You could probably travel it in a couple of days on horseback."

"If he did," I speculated, "then the second Richard Ausby might want the land because he thinks the loot is still there."

"But it's not for sale," Drew argued.

"And it's full of lead contamination," I added. "So why would he want it?" I paused. "Unless...he's the one who is contaminating it!"

"Why would he do *that*?" Drew looked at me as if I had scrambled eggs for brains.

"Don't you see?" I said excitedly. "If he could prove that the land was contaminated, then there would be no point in having a park there. The plaque on the bench said that the lady who owned the homestead willed it to the city specifically for a recreation area. The only way he could get his hands on that land would be if it were unfit for public use."

"That still doesn't explain why he'd want it if it was contaminated," Drew said.

"The guy I talked to on the phone who was in charge of the testing told me that the lead had only been found in a few isolated areas and not near the home site, which he thought was weird. Ausby could easily be planting lead so the tests are positive. Then he could clean up the contaminated spots after he buys the land."

"That still doesn't completely explain why he wants it," said Drew.

"The house and the barns were destroyed in a fire. If the first Ausby hid the loot in the cellar or buried it somewhere on the property, it might still be there. But this Richard Ausby has no way of knowing where the heck it is. How is he supposed to go into a city park and start shoveling? The only way he'd have the time he needs is if he owned the land."

"Okay, that makes sense," Drew conceded. "But the missing loot would have to be worth millions to justify all this."

"Maybe it is. Who knows?" I said. My social studies teacher was glaring in my direction. "Meet me at the park after school, okay? We'll look for clues," I whispered.

chapter eleven

"Something just doesn't add up here," Julia complained as she tripped over a tree root. I'd explained everything to her on the way to the park. "Why would this Ausby guy threaten me on my cell phone? I can see him vandalizing the soccer nets and contaminating the soil, but what good would it do for him to target me?"

"I have no idea, but he might have gotten hold of your cell phone number through your mom," I said. "Maybe it was just a way of distracting us so we wouldn't pick up on the other stuff."

"Hmmphf." Julia didn't sound convinced.

The park was quiet. I couldn't see Drew anywhere.

"Isn't that him? Over there in the trees?" Julia pointed.

I looked. "I don't think so." The figure paused, and then it disappeared further into the brush.

"Maybe it's Ausby." Julia shivered.

"I doubt he'd be snooping around here in broad daylight," I said.

"Why not? We are," Julia pointed out.

"Let's check out the bench. I want to be sure about the name." I trotted over to the park bench, ignoring the warning signs that instructed people to stay out of the park. The bench was still in the same place, and the sign was very clear.

"I was right. Her name was Denise Ausby," I said in triumph.

"That doesn't prove much." Drew came up behind me.

"No, but it means my theory might not be totally wrong, either," I said.

Drew held his hands up in surrender. "Hey, I'm not picking on you. I'm just not sure I believe that someone would deliberately contaminate soil so they could buy land."

A crackling in the underbrush made us all freeze. My heart leaped into my throat, and in spite of what I'd said to Julia, I had visions of Richard Ausby coming after us with a heavy shovel in his hands.

Instead, a different man burst through the bushes carrying a number of small plastic containers. He stopped. "What are you kids doing here? Didn't you see the signs?"

"We just needed to check something," I said. "Are you one of the city testers?"

He nodded. "I'm Bob Greene. I'm in charge of the operation. And you kids better clear out of here. It looks like we're going to have to close the park. Permanently."

chapter twelve

Julia bent over her soccer bag and checked her cell phone for the fifth time. "Still nothing."

"Is it on?" I tightened the laces on my cleats.

"Yeah." Julia tossed it back in the bag.

No threats so far, I thought. I watched the action on the field. Our players struggled to get the ball—the other team had amazing passing skills, and they seemed to know each other's positions on the field at all times. I could tell that we would need to play our absolute best in order to have any hope of winning this game.

Coach Collins studied the other team grimly. "Okay, girls," he said. "I need you to dive in there and get the ball. You have to be one hundred percent fearless, all right? This team is aggressive, and they are going to do whatever it takes to keep possession. Julia, once you have it, take the shot as soon as you get the opportunity. Don't wait. Okay?"

She nodded.

"Izzy, your job is to feed the ball to Julia. You're a fast runner; if you can get ahead of everyone and slam a goal in there, great. But if you're blocked, look for Julia. She'll be trying to get clear. All right?"

"Okay," I answered.

"Good. Get out there." Coach motioned for a shift change.

I ran out on the field with Julia right behind me. Nicola was on this line as well, which didn't strike me as a good idea after what happened last time. Then I put it out of my mind and focused on the game.

The girl I had to cover was quick; she could run in such fast bursts that I had to fight to keep up. She got the ball and thundered down into our end. I sprinted after her. I knew I was out of position, but I didn't want to leave our defense without support.

I caught up with her and dug for the ball, trying to smash it sideways and get it out of her control. She dodged me twice, but I finally got a piece of it and sent the ball toward the sideline.

Nicola appeared out of nowhere and scooped it up. She raced up the field, dribbling the ball, just keeping it inbounds.

"Izzy! Get back!" Coach yelled from the sidelines.

I galloped after Nicola. A bunch of their players swarmed her as she neared the goal, but I was still open.

"Nicola, pass back!" Coach hollered.

I could see Julia positioning herself near the net. If Nicola passed it back to me, I could dodge the players who surrounded Nicola and slam a quick pass to Julia. She would have a perfect shot.

"Nicola!" I shouted.

Nicola fought to get through the players who blocked her shot on the net.

"Nicola, pass it back!" Coach's voice took on a frantic note.

I was still clear, but not for long. My heart pounded, and I felt the familiar tightening in my stomach. What if I messed up yet again?

But I never had the chance to find out. My opponent with the lightning feet had reached me and began to cover me. One of the players who was covering Nicola dug the ball out of the swarm and Lightening Feet was on it immediately. She took off down the field, darting around me and sprinting toward our goalie.

I groaned inwardly and once again dashed down the field. But it was too late. Ashley, our goalie, had the stricken look of a gopher caught in headlights as Lightning Feet charged her like a locomotive. Ashley didn't have a chance as the ball found the upper corner of the net.

The whistle blew. Coach motioned us off for the switch. Dispirited, I ran off.

The minute our line was off the field, Coach laid into Nicola.

"Why didn't you pass back like I told you?" he demanded.

"I didn't hear you," Nicola said sullenly.

"The whole world could hear him, he was yelling so loud," Julia snapped. "So why couldn't you?"

"Look, just butt out, Julia," Nicola yelled.

"Stop it, girls," Coach said. "Nicola, you need to be thinking out there, okay? If you had passed back to Izzy, she had a clear pass to Julia, who was right in front of the net. Next time, don't try to fight through all those players. You probably cost us a goal back there. Pass to someone. Okay?"

Nicola nodded and turned away. She rummaged through her soccer bag for her water bottle. I ignored her and went over to Julia, who was slugging back her own water. I still wasn't happy with Nicola for chatting up Drew at school, and I definitely wasn't thrilled with her attitude on the team.

"She's really starting to bug me," Julia said angrily.

"Forget it. We need to focus on the game. We're down two goals now," I said.

Julia threw her water bottle down onto her bag. The plastic top popped off, and water gushed into the bag through the open zipper.

"Aggh!" Julia knelt down and grabbed the bottle. She dumped the contents of her bag out. Her cell phone, fleece jacket and extra soccer gear were soaked. "Well, that's just great." Julia surveyed the mess. "I hope the phone still works." She picked it up. It vibrated in her hand. She looked up at me. "There's a message."

I tensed. "What does it say?"

Julia clicked a button, and then instead of watching the tiny screen, she listened to a voice message. She smiled and shut the phone off. "It was from my mom. She's going to be a few minutes late picking us up from the game," she said in relief.

"That's okay," I said. "I'm glad it wasn't our cyber stalker."

"Me too." Julia picked up her wet jacket and the soccer gear and shoved them back inside the bag. A soggy piece of paper fell to the ground.

"What's that?" I said. I picked it up.

"I don't know," answered Julia. "Probably an old notice or something."

I smoothed it out and held it up, dripping. "Uh, no. It's not." I showed her the words, scribbled in pencil.

Stay out of the way, cherry-picker.
Soccer's a rough game. You might get hurt.

"Now Ausby's sending me notes?" Julia said. "But he's not even here! How could he have put this in my bag?"

"Exactly." I folded the paper carefully. "He couldn't. Because Ausby's not the guy."

"What!" Julia blinked. "But you said that Ausby was targeting our soccer team to get the land."

"Uh...no. I think Ausby vandalized our nets before he came up with the idea to contaminate the soil and fool all of us into thinking the park was unsafe. But now I'm pretty sure he's not the guy who's been threatening you. It's someone else."

"So now we're back to someone from

another team who wants to scare us out of the playoffs?" Julia threw her hands up. "That's like looking for a needle in a haystack. It could take forever to figure out who it is."

"No," I said thoughtfully, "I don't think so. I have a pretty good idea who it is."

"Really?" Julia said with exaggerated patience. "Well, would you mind telling me, or do you want to wait until next season?"

I lowered my voice. "It's Nicola."

chapter thirteen

"Nicola!" Julia nearly shouted.

Nicola turned at the sound of her name and glared in our direction.

"Shh!" I cautioned.

"What do you mean, it's Nicola?" Julia whispered.

"Look at this note. She calls you a cherry-picker. She's called you that name before. And it's handwritten in pencil. How many adults would do something dumb like that? Handwriting can be traced."

"So we're going to swipe Nicola's homework or something, so we can compare the handwriting?" Julia asked.

"No, I don't think we'll need to. If we can get her cell phone, we can check the log of calls. If your number is on there with the dates and times that you received those threats, I think that will prove it."

"How are you going to get it?" Julia wanted to know.

"I saw it in her soccer bag. Wait here." I walked over to the heap of sports bags and began to rummage through them, pretending to look for my own. Nicola's was nearby. I nudged it with my foot until it was in the middle of several bags, pulled my own over top, and then I reached down with my hand. It looked like I had my hand in my own bag, but instead I was searching through Nicola's. I groped for the phone. When I found it, I drew it out and quickly stashed it in my own bag. Then I pulled out my water bottle and took a drink, so it looked like I'd been searching for that all along. I brought the bag over to where Julia was waiting.

"Did you get it?" she asked.

I nodded. "Check the log. Quick, it's almost half-time." Julia and I were the only ones not paying any attention to the game. We were down three goals to one. Everyone else's eyes were riveted to the field, including Nicola's.

Julia was pressing buttons. "I'm not sure," she muttered. "This phone's a bit different from mine..." She tried again. "Got it!" she said.

"Show me." I looked at the little, brightly lit screen. It showed a list of numbers and the times the text messages were sent. Julia's number was on there several times. "Bingo!" I said triumphantly. "All we have to do is match those times with calls your phone received, and we've got her."

At that moment, half-time was called. As our team members trotted off the field, sweaty and tired from the shift, Nicola glanced in our direction. Then she saw Julia holding two phones and her eyes widened.

"Hey! Give me that!" she snarled. She leaped over the pile of soccer bags and tried to wrench the phone from Julia's hand. "What do you think you're doing?"

Julia hung on, twisting out of Nicola's grip. "Checking to see what phone calls you've been making lately. Too bad you didn't delete them, Nicola. All the evidence is right here." She stepped away and held the phone out of Nicola's reach.

Nicola's face paled, but she said, "I have no idea what you're talking about."

"Oh, I think you do." Julia's voice was menacing.

"What's going on here?" Coach strode over.

"I've been getting a bunch of text message threats on my cell phone. Izzy and I just found proof that it's Nicola who's been doing it."

"I did not!" Nicola fired back.

"What!" Coach's voice was shocked.

"Look at this." Julia showed Coach the messages that she had saved on her cell phone and the note we'd found in her soccer bag.

"How do you know Nicola is the one responsible?" he asked.

"Exactly!" Nicola spat.

Julia just smiled. "Because of this." She held up Nicola's phone.

"Give me back my phone!" Nicola tried again to grab it.

Coach held up his hand. "Wait, Nicola."

Julia showed him the call log on Nicola's phone. "Those calls were placed at the same time my phone received the threats. And that's my cell phone number right there."

Coach's face was grave. "That's some pretty strong evidence, Nicola. What do you have to say?"

Nicola swallowed. "There was a scout for the national team at some of the games, and I figured that if Julia was too scared to play, then maybe I'd finally have a chance."

"A scout? Who told you that?" Coach Collins asked, puzzled.

"Izzy did." Nicola scowled.

Coach looked at me. I held up my hands. "Hey, I never told her anything. We were just guessing, because there was this guy in a tie, with a clipboard, hanging around. It turned out he wasn't a scout at all."

"So you admit to sending these messages to Julia?" Coach pressed.

Nicola seemed to wilt. "Yeah, but I just wanted a chance to show what I could do. Everyone always thinks Julia's the best."

"Hey, Coach! Half-time's over. Are you guys going to play this game or what?" the young ref yelled from the field.

"Okay!" Coach called back. "Second line, go out there again. I need to deal with something here." He turned back to us. "Julia, you should have told me what was happening. As your coach, that's part of my job."

Julia nodded, but Nicola looked away, her lips compressed.

"And Nicola, you're riding the bench for the rest of the game. I have no choice but to discuss this whole incident with your parents and suspend you from the team."

chapter fourteen

Julia and Drew slid their lunch bags along the table and plunked themselves into the chairs I'd saved beside me. I chewed on a carrot stick, thinking so hard I barely noticed them.

"Okay, Iz," Drew said. "What's the deal?"

"This whole thing with our soccer field is really bugging me," I said. "Now that we know Nicola was the one threatening Julia, we've got to prove that Richard Ausby is the person who's vandalizing the park area."

"Why?" Julia wanted to know. "Why don't we just let the police handle it?"

"Oh, come on." I snorted. "Do you really think the police are going to believe us instead of some rich business guy? Ausby's going to end up getting away with it."

"But how do you know Nicola didn't vandalize the park?" asked Drew. "Just because she didn't confess to it..."

"Give me a break. She could have sliced the soccer nets, maybe, but why would she? Nicola's whole motive was to get Julia to play badly so she could show her up. Vandalizing the nets wouldn't help with that at all. Neither would contaminating the soil—and that's assuming she would even know how to do it," I said.

"If we only knew whether the loot from that train robbery you guys told me about was really buried at that homestead, then we might have something," said Julia.

Drew ran his hand through his hair, making it stand up on end. "That's got to be impossible. The train robbery was nearly ninety years ago. How are you going to find out anything now? The people who were involved with it are all dead!"

"Yeah," I said slowly. "But stories like that get passed down in families. Maybe someone besides Richard from the Ausby family is still alive."

"The plaque at the park didn't say that Denise Ausby was the last one of the family," Drew pointed out.

"Even if she was the last one of the family to live on that land," I argued. "that doesn't mean she didn't have relatives somewhere."

"Yeah, but how are you going to find them?" Drew countered.

I frowned. "I don't know."

"Uh...you could try looking up Ausby in the phone book," Julia suggested.

Drew and I looked at each other. I started to laugh. "That's so obvious. Why didn't I think of that?"

"There's a phone book at the office," said Julia.

"Let's go check." Drew shoved his chair back, the remnants of his sandwich still in one hand.

We followed him out the cafeteria door and down the hall to the phone outside the school office. A phone book inside a vinyl binder was attached to a shelf under the phone. I grabbed it first and immediately began thumbing through the *A* section.

"Astor, Atkins, Atwell," I muttered.

Julia peered over my shoulder. "Did you find it?"

"Ausby!" I pointed to the name. "There are only a few listed. Do you think we should phone now?"

"Why not?" Drew picked up the receiver. "But be careful what you say. They aren't going to reveal family secrets about buried treasure to a stranger over the phone."

I took a deep breath and dialed. The phone rang three times before an answering machine clicked in. I hung up without saying anything. "No one was home," I said. I tried the next number.

"Hello?" The young woman's voice sounded impatient. A baby was bawling in the background.

"Hi," I said nervously. "This is Isabella

MacAllister calling. I'm looking for someone who might have some information—"

"Not interested," the woman interrupted.

"No, wait! Please don't hang up! I'm not selling anything. It's about Denise Ausby's land!"

"Denise? She's dead."

"I know that!" I persisted. "But I need to find out about something that happened a long time ago on that farm."

The woman paused. I could still hear the baby shrieking. "Just a minute." I waited. The woman hollered, "Brent! Give that kid her bottle and c'mere. Some girl on the phone wants to know about your Great Aunt Denise."

There was a clattering as the phone was laid down, followed by a sudden silence. I waited again, and within a few moments a man's voice answered.

"Hello?" he said.

"Hi," I said. I repeated my name and why I was calling.

"Aunt Denise left that land to the city about five years ago. None of us saw a penny." The young man didn't sound bitter, just matter-of-fact. "I don't know much about it."

"Is there anyone left in your family who might be able to talk to me?" I asked desperately.

"Nope. Not really. Just my grandma, but she's in a nursing home. She's not all there, you know. Goes nuts, sometimes."

"Would it be okay if I talked to her anyway?" I held my breath.

"Sure. Won't do you any good, but you can try. Her name's Edith Ausby. She's in the Broadview Nursing Home. You'll have to ask for her at the front desk, and the nurse will take you in."

"Thank you," I said gratefully and hung up.

chapter fifteen

"Edith! Edith, you have a young visitor today," the nurse sang out cheerfully, in a voice loud enough to shake the rafters. The old woman sitting in a chair by the window didn't move, but continued to stare out into the bright, shifting sunlight that filtered through the birch tree outside.

The nurse patted my shoulder. "Just speak up, and you'll be fine. I have to go and check on some of the other residents."

My heart sank. How was I supposed to get secrets out of this person by yelling at the top of my lungs? So much for keeping the information confidential—the entire nursing home would hear.

The old woman had a faded shrunken look, like someone's favorite rag doll that had been forgotten outside for the entire summer. Her shriveled face was deeply wrinkled, her sparse gray hair curled at random, her purplish cardigan and flowered dress were ragged and shapeless. The whole room smelled of old wool and floor cleaner.

At first I felt a pang of sympathy for this old lady whose mind was unhinged, who had to be shouted at to be heard, who had nothing better to do than stare out a window all day. But then she turned to face me, and I saw her sharp eyes and the intelligence in her glance.

"Who are you?" she asked.

"Isabella MacAllister," I yelled.

"You needn't shout, Isabella. In spite of what they think, I am not as deaf as a post. I just choose what I want to hear." Her eyes twinkled. She motioned to a second chair near the window. "Come and sit down. Are you here for a school project? I'm almost ninety-five, you know. I could tell you stories of the days before computers that you likely wouldn't believe."

"No, I haven't come because of school. It's about some land that your family used to own. Denise Ausby's land."

"Denise? My sister-in-law? That used to be my husband's family farm."

"I was wondering if you could tell me about Richard Ausby," I said.

"Which one? My good-for-nothing great-nephew or the train robber?" Edith answered.

I fought to keep a smile from breaking on my face. She knew both! "Um, I'd like to hear about each of them, actually."

Edith regarded me astutely. "You know more than you're telling, I'll wager. How about you tell me *your* stories, first."

I took a deep breath. "Well, my friends and I think that Richard Ausby—the one living now—is trying to buy the land that your sister-in-law Denise left to the city."

Edith frowned. "But Denise specified that the land was to be used for a park. It wasn't supposed to be sold."

"I know. But I think Richard is deliberately contaminating the soil in the park with lead, so that the city will say it's not safe for the public. And if it's not safe, then it can't be used as a park."

"And Richard could contest the will and buy the land," Edith finished. "That sounds like him, all right." She rubbed a finger thoughtfully on her chin. "But why do you think he wants it? He could end up in a legal tangle that could take years before the purchase is cleared."

"That depends on what you know about the first Richard Ausby," I said. "I think that he may have come home and hidden the loot from the robbery on the farm before he escaped to the United States. I'm guessing that Richard the Second figured this out, and he wants the land so he can search for the loot. Either that, or he wants to have the park closed so that he can search without worrying too much about being interrupted."

"I'd say you're a pretty smart cookie, Isabella. I think you're exactly right. And I can tell you that I remember that robbery as clear as day. I was eight years old, and my folks farmed just outside of Calgary at the time. The robbery was big news. No one knew for sure that Richard made it back to his brother's place—the farm that you're talking about. But after I married William Ausby in 1932, I heard plenty of rumors, let me tell you."

"Did anyone ever tell you where the loot was buried?" I asked eagerly.

"Who says it was buried?" Edith demanded.

"Well, it must be. The house and barns burned to the ground. If the treasure was hidden there, it would have been destroyed years ago," I faltered.

"Maybe. But isn't that the first place the police would look?" said Edith.

"Probably," I answered. "I guess I didn't think of that."

"And just what would you do with the

stolen jewelry if you found it?" Edith asked.

"Take it to the police," I said promptly. "And use it to stop the second Richard Ausby from ruining the park and my soccer field."

Edith gave me a sharp look. "I believe you're an honest girl. I've kept a secret for many years now, but I'm getting old. Maybe now is the time to let it go." She settled back in her chair. "So it's my turn for stories now." She smiled as she remembered. "James Ausby farmed the land that is now the park, while his brother Richard went off to work the mines in the Crowsnest Pass. Richard hooked up with those other two men and robbed the train in 1920. I heard that Richard had most of the loot—including a fabulous ruby necklace that one of the rumrunners on the train was bringing to the girl he intended to marry."

"Why didn't the other two guys take their share?" I asked.

"I don't know. Maybe they sent Richard to hide it, thinking that the three of them would split it up later. As it turned out, the other men didn't live long enough—one was killed in a shootout with police in a café in Bellevue a few days after the robbery. The second man escaped into the rocks of the Frank Slide."

"What happened then?" I said.

"Well, they had a devil of a time finding him—those rocks are piled so high—they're like a maze. They got him a few days later, though, at Pincher Station. He couldn't stay in that rocky area for long—a man needs to eat, you know. They jailed him—this was in August—and they hanged him in December. So Richard Ausby never did see those men again.

"Back on the farm, James Ausby had had three sons—Jimmy, William and Thomas. Jimmy was the oldest, and he married Denise the year before I married William. Jimmy took over the farm from his dad, but this was during the Depression. Jobs were hard to find, so Will and I moved onto the farm for a time as well. And that's when I heard the rumors."

I held my breath.

"Folks in town said that Richard *had* made

it home. Then my mother-in-law let it slip one time that the loot had been buried under the roots of an old pine tree, because the police had come and searched the house."

"Why didn't James turn over the loot to the police?" I asked.

"Well, for two reasons. One, he didn't want to see his brother jailed or hanged. And two, he'd likely get himself into trouble as well, for keeping stolen property and protecting a criminal."

"Did you ever check the pine tree?" I asked eagerly.

"Yes, several of them. And I didn't find a thing."

Crestfallen, I slumped against the back of the chair. But Edith leaned forward.

"I think if the jewels and money had been hidden in the tree, by the time I came along they'd long since been moved. Don't forget, this is a good twelve years or so after the robbery, and Richard died in prison in 1926 without ever telling anyone what he did with the stolen treasure. I think James moved it somewhere safer after all the hoopla died down."

"Do you know where?" I said.

"No, but I have a guess. We used to ground-store some of the crops—potatoes and carrots and so forth—"

"Didn't you have a refrigerator?" I interrupted.

Edith laughed. "No, we had an icebox instead, but it wasn't big enough to store everything. Ground storage helped keep some things fresh for longer. It was a short trench, like a shallow cellar. It was dug a little ways from the house and lined with stones inside. James had built a little wooden platform with a trapdoor over top. At harvest time, we filled the cellar full, then laid dirt and sod over the platform to keep the vegetables cool. It was very clever, really. The grass grew right over it, so you had to know exactly where that handle was in order to pull up the door and reach down to get what you needed for supper.

"One day the trap door stuck, and I yanked a bit too hard. We were only supposed to open it about halfway, just enough to reach inside, because of course the sod might fall off if you opened it all the way. Well, that's exactly what happened. The sod came flying off that old door and there I was, in a clean housedress, with hunks of muddy dirt and grass all over me. Was I mad! Laundry in those days was no picnic.

"With the door open wide, I could see inside the cellar. As I grabbed the potatoes I was after for our dinner, I spotted an old cast-iron kettle tucked way in the back corner. I thought that was an odd thing to be in there, so—since I couldn't get much dirtier—I climbed down to have a look."

"What was in there?" I questioned.

"An old sack, rolled up tight. And then I heard my father-in-law coming, so I climbed up, quick as a wink, and shut the trapdoor. James was plenty mad when he saw the mess and gave me one of the worst tongue-lashings I'd ever had. Made me think twice about going back to have another look—but it also made me think there was more to the story than he was telling."

"Did you ever check the ground cellar

again?"

Edith shook her head. "No, a few months later Will got work in Edmonton, and we moved. Then we had our children, and I was too busy, even when we did get back down to this neck of the woods."

"Do you think it was the ruby necklace? Do you think it's still there?" I asked.

"Could be," said Edith.

"Could you tell me exactly where the cellar was?"

"It was about one hundred yards west of the house. The barns were to the east. I'll draw you a little map." Edith reached for a pen and a scrap of paper.

"Who's this other Richard guy?" I said.

Edith snorted. "He's my great-nephew. Jimmy and Denise had a daughter, but she died about twenty years ago. So the only descendants to that land were my children and my brother-in-law Thomas's grandson, Richard. Richard's father—Thomas's son—died when Richard was just a baby. There wasn't much money in the estate. My grandson Brent got some furniture and small things—he was planning to have a garage sale, but he's not much of an up-and-comer. I think all that junk is in his garage yet. But that Richard is a slimy good-for-nothing whose only concern is money. I had no objection at all when Denise wanted to leave the land for public use. Better that than have young Richard put a stack of condominiums on it."

"Do you think Richard knows about the train robbery?"

"Oh, certainly. The story was notorious in the family. That ruby necklace was supposed to be priceless at the time. Add the historical value today, and it would be worth millions."

"Does he know about the ground cellar?"

"I don't think so. James kept his mouth closed about it. Richard asked me about the robbery once or twice, but I knew the sort of things he'd get up to, so I never told anyone." Edith winked. "Until today."

chapter sixteen

"So she doesn't know for sure that the loot is there?" Drew shifted his backpack. It clanked in response, and he winced as something hard dug into his spine. "Iz, can you move some of that stuff? One of the shovels in there is killing me."

I took hold of one of the handles that was sticking out of the top and pulled it out. Drew, Julia and I had been on our way back to the park, but I'd convinced them to take a detour after school—via the bus—to Ausby's neighborhood. I knew that finding the treasure alone wouldn't be enough to prove that Ausby had been deliberately contaminating the park. We would need evidence...

So here we were, armed with a bunch of garden tools, some small shovels, and an edger to cut through the sod. But treasure hunting would have to wait.

"No, but it's the best lead we have," I replied. "What other choice do we have? We could dig around the ruins for the next ten years and still find nothing."

"That must be what Richard Ausby's going to do," Julia commented. "Since he doesn't know where the loot is either."

"We don't know that," Drew corrected. "And the guy would have to be pretty stupid if he plans to dig through the entire farm. No, I bet he has some idea. Why else would this whole thing about buying the land suddenly come up? Why wouldn't he have brought it up when his aunt died five years ago?"

"I don't think he had the money then. Besides, he had to have a reason to contest the will." The thought worried me. We had to get to that cellar before him. But there was something we had to do first.

"What's the house number, again?" I asked Julia.

"It's 521. It should be down the next block." Julia consulted the page I'd torn from a public phone book.

"Let's just walk casually down the front first, then sneak down the alley around back," I suggested.

Drew snorted. "Walk casually? With enough tools to start a gold-mining operation?"

I ignored him and strode purposefully down the sidewalk. The street where Richard Ausby lived was pleasant and tree-lined, with renovated two-story houses butted up against old war-time bungalows. Ausby's house looked expensive, with steel gray stucco and brick trim. No flowers adorned the patches of shrubbery.

"That's it—521," I said.

"Come on. Let's go before he gets home. He's probably at work," Julia suggested.

"Exactly." I led the way down the block to the alley entrance. We slipped along the fence line, until we reached a fence that was painted the same color as Ausby's house.

"Is this it?" I asked. "We have to be one hundred percent sure."

Drew took hold of the fence and jumped, peering over the top. "Yeah, this is it."

"Okay. Quick, give me the gloves."

Julia drew a pair of rubber gloves out of her backpack. "This is going to be so gross!" she said.

I put on the gloves and grabbed the first bag of trash that was sitting inside the metal garbage can. I untied it carefully and winced as the smell of fish guts wafted up from the plastic. "Eeuuw!" I gagged. I reached down and shifted the mass of trash, but it was mostly kitchen scraps and pieces of paper. I churned the paper upward and handed a soggy sheaf of it to Drew. "See if there's anything in there we can use," I told him.

He took it gingerly, holding it between two

gloved fingers. Julia so far had refused to put her gloves on. "What am I looking for?"

"Anything to do with the soil contamination or the park. Receipts, anything," I replied. I tied up the trash bag and moved on to the next one. This one made a tinkling noise, like broken glass. I was careful as I opened it. Sure enough, there were shards of glass scattered through another mass of papers and used Kleenex. I winced at that thought, but I reached down cautiously and took hold of the one glass container that was still intact. It had a grayish silty residue on the inside. I took it out.

"Julia, I need a Ziploc bag," I said. She held it open, and I eased the jar inside.

"Do you think this is evidence?" she asked.

"I don't know. But it looks a bit like metal, so maybe it's lead. The police would have to test it."

"I found something!" Drew whispered in excitement. "Look, you guys. It's part of a printout from an alchemy website." He pointed to the heading. The page was torn, but the words *sugar of lead* were clear in one corner.

I took the damp smelly piece of paper from him. "That's great!" I congratulated him. "We need to keep it separate, though." Julia presented me with another plastic bag, which she carefully sealed and added to her backpack.

I reached into the second trash bag again, and down near the bottom I saw a bright yellow rubber glove. I reached for it, but just then Julia grabbed my arm.

"I heard someone!" she squeaked.

I jumped. I felt a shard of glass pierce my glove. "Ow!" I exclaimed.

"Let's get out of here!" Drew whispered.

"Just a minute." I peered inside the bag and gently grabbed the yellow glove. It had a shiny grayish film on it, just like the inside of the jar. "Put this in a bag, quick." I dumped it into a third bag, quickly tied up the trash, stuffed my gloves inside my own backpack and began walking down the alley.

Drew and Julia were right behind me. "Don't run," I murmured. "People will get suspicious. Just pretend we're walking home from school."

"Do you think he saw us?" Julia worried.

Her question was answered as the gate swung open back at Ausby's. We were only about four houses away, but someone had parked a big camper behind the house. "Duck!" yelled Drew. The three of us dodged behind the RV. I peered around the corner.

A green plastic garbage bag was tossed out to join the ones we had just searched. Then the gate slammed shut. I let out a huge sigh. "I guess he didn't see us."

"It wasn't even him. It was a woman," Drew said.

"Maybe it's a cleaning lady. Or a girlfriend," I suggested. I cast a longing look at the new garbage bag, but Drew took my arm.

"You're bleeding," he said. "And we've got enough for now. Ausby could get home any minute."

"I don't think so," I answered, examining the cut on my finger. "I know where he is."

"Where?" Drew and Julia said together.

"At the park, digging for the loot from the train robbery." I fixed them with a determined stare.

"And that's where we're going next!"

chapter seventeen

"Izzy, I'm starving," Drew complained. The bus pulled away in a puff of exhaust.

"After those fish heads?" Julia pretended to gag. "You have to be kidding."

"And you need to clean that cut," Drew insisted.

"Drew's right," Julia said. "Besides, we should store this trash you saved somewhere safe."

"Oh, all right." I gave in. "I just don't want Ausby to find the loot ahead of us."

We traipsed into my house, the tools clanking. Drew set his backpack down in relief. "At last! Can I have something to eat?"

"I'll ask." I went into the kitchen and washed my hands with disinfectant soap. My mom was nowhere to be seen, so I grabbed a bunch of bananas from the bowl on the table and headed for the front door.

"That's it?" Drew said when I handed him the bananas.

"Be grateful," I told him. "If I had my way, we'd already be digging. Come on, let's go."

Drew rolled his eyes, peeled a banana and took a huge bite.

"Izzy?" Julia plucked a scrap of paper that was taped to the closet door. "Did you see this?"

"What?" I reached for it.

"It's a note from your mom," Julia said grimly.

My eyes widened at the name scribbled on the note. *Edith Ausby called.* Next to it was the message, *He knows*. Mom had put big question marks next to it, but I ignored her written request to call her and let her know what was going on.

I felt my stomach tighten. Ausby must have gone to see Edith again. Had he threatened her? He knew she didn't like him, but he must have gotten the information out of her somehow. Now the race to find the treasure had just gotten a whole lot faster.

I scrawled a note to Mom. *At the park. Might be late for supper.* Then I taped it to the closet and grabbed my backpack. "Come on, you guys!"

"Just a sec." Julia shoved the plastic bags of trash into my soccer bag, which was sitting inside the closet; then she zipped it shut. She and Drew followed. "We'll hide that stuff somewhere better when we get back."

We walked around the soccer field, coming into the natural area from the back way. This had to be a quick and thorough search. I'd described what Edith had told me, and we had the map. The key was going to be finding the entrance to the root cellar, if it still existed. Otherwise we were going to try to pinpoint where the cellar had been and start digging.

"Keep an eye out for him," I whispered softly to Drew. He nodded, his mouth a grim line. I parted the bushes with my hands and stepped onto a narrow path that led up through the copse of trees growing on the hillside. The memorial bench was up at the top, at the far end of the home site. According to Edith's map, the root cellar was west of the original house.

"The soccer field and ball diamond are on the north end of the park, right?" I murmured.

"Yeah." Drew was right behind me on the path.

"So we need to go left from here, if we can find a path." I looked with despair at the tangle of wild rose bushes, sharp with thorns, that lined the trail at this point. "We're not getting through there."

"Maybe they'll thin out nearer the top," Drew suggested. "Keep going."

I reached the top of the hill and squatted down in the bushes, crawling to the edge of the trees to peek through. There was no sign of Richard Ausby anywhere. The park was deserted.

"It's all clear," I whispered back to Drew and Julia. Drew crawled alongside me and glanced around as well.

"We have to go that way." He pointed. "See that little rise in the ground? I bet that's it."

"It's right in the open." I bit my lip. "We'll have to keep watch."

We got to our feet and, with one more glance around, snuck out of our hiding place.

I laid down my backpack when we reached the rise of earth Drew had pointed out. "Look for a handle, what's left of the platform, anything that would tell us where the root cellar used to be," I told Julia. "It might have caved in when the bulldozers were in here making the park."

I kicked at the tufts of grass that grew along the rise, then pulled on my rubber gloves and got down on my hands and knees, feeling for an iron ring, an edge of wood. Drew did the same, but I stopped Julia.

"Jules, can you keep a lookout?" I asked. "Hide in the bushes over there and watch for Ausby. I have a weird feeling."

"It's because of that phone call," Julia said. But she took her backpack and crouched underneath a bush, hidden in the tall grass. Drew and I carried on, but we didn't find anything except wild prairie grass and an anthill. I stripped off a glove and rubbed my forehead with one sweaty hand.

"I wish we knew where the lead contamination is," I commented.

"I think we do," Drew said. "I noticed red flags hammered into the ground in places, back near the soccer field. I bet that's where they've found it."

"So that means that this soil is clean," I said.

"Maybe," Drew answered. "But keep your gloves on."

"I know," I said, irritated. "I just meant that Ausby probably wouldn't contaminate the soil where he planned to dig."

"Not likely," Drew agreed.

"Let's keep going," I sighed. We moved off the rise and down into a hollow.

"She said it was on a little hill," I objected, when Drew started to search.

"Yeah, but there were bulldozers and stuff in here when they made the park. What if the cellar caved in?"

"It might have," I said. "But remember, they left this part pretty much as it was, except for clearing off the buildings," I said, but I dropped down beside him anyway and carefully felt along the roots of the grasses. There was nothing more than dirt and rocks. I squatted on my heels and looked at the millions of grass stems waving in the wind. The root cellar could be anywhere. We were close, according to the map, but Edith was old. What if she had remembered it wrong?

I gritted my teeth in frustration. The thing had to be here somewhere. I crept forward and began working more quickly, covering the ground faster. As I crawled out of the hollow onto a flatter area, a pointed rock dug into the knee of my jeans.

"Yow!" I rubbed the bruised area, annoyed. Then I took a second look.

I couldn't see a rock. But my throbbing knee was clear evidence that something hard and sharp was there. I stripped off my gloves.

There, in a gap between clumps of grass, was a broken hinge. I scraped away the dirt and roots to find a very old piece of wood. My mouth was dry.

"Drew!" I croaked. "I think it's here!"

Drew knelt beside me, feeling for the end of the platform. I traced the edges with my fingers until I could feel the clasp of the trapdoor, half-buried in the dirt.

"Did you find it?" Julia was suddenly looking over my shoulder. In answer I gave a gentle heave on the ring of the clasp, and the trapdoor raised slightly before the clasp came away in my hand. What was left of the door fell back with a muffled thud.

"The wood must be completely rotten," I gasped.

"Dig," Drew said, handing me a shovel.

The three of us dug into the soil around

the door, lifting the old door up and throwing it back on its hinges.

The smell of damp earthy decay seeped from the cavity below.

"Eeeuuw! I bet that place is just full of slugs." Julia grimaced.

Drew and I eagerly looked down. With the trapdoor fully open, the cellar was really an oblong pit, about three feet deep and six feet long. The trapdoor in the center made it fairly easy to reach into the pit, and a long-forgotten tin bucket was within arm's reach.

Drew grabbed the flashlight from one of the backpacks and flicked it on. He shone it into the gloomy corners. "See anything?" he asked.

"What's that?" I pointed to a blackish thing pushed so far into one end it was half-hidden in the dirt-and-stone wall.

"I can't tell." Drew played the light over the object. I could make out that it was round, and...there was a spout on one side.

"It's there!" The breath seemed to rush out of me in one gasp. "Keep the light on it.

I'm going in." I eased my body over the edge. The pit was so low I had to get down on my belly to reach the object. I tried not to think about what Julia had said about slugs.

I touched it—it *was* a kettle—and the cast-iron was so heavy I could barely move it. I used two hands to drag it toward me, and then I lifted it into Drew's hands. Julia helped me up through the trapdoor.

"Hurry! Open it," I said.

"I can't. The lid's rusted. It's stuck." Drew grunted with effort as he tried to pry it loose.

"Here. Let me try." Julia took the flat side of the edger and jimmied the lid. "Izzy, help me," she said. Carefully we wiggled the lid until Drew was able to pull it off.

I reached inside.

chapter eighteen

I pulled gently at the tightly wadded sacking wedged in the bottom of the kettle. The kettle's spout had been jammed with some type of clay, so the material was dirty and rust-stained but not wet. Someone had packed this well, considering there was no plastic wrap at the time.

The sack was disintegrating as I tugged.

"Just let it rip," Julia said.

"If she does, I'm outta here," Drew joked.

Julia snorted. "I meant the fabric, bozo."

I focused on the sacking. It came loose with a soft tearing sound, and I drew it through the kettle's opening.

Drew and Julia leaned over. I unfolded the cloth, and there, among several gold watches and a number of coins, was the ruby necklace. It was clogged with dirt but still sparkled as I held it up.

"Wow," Julia breathed.

"It's pretty big," Drew touched the stones. "I wonder what it's worth."

"Far too much for you," a menacing voice said from behind us.

The three of us swiveled instantly. I swallowed hard. Richard Ausby was no more than ten feet away. My nerveless fingers dropped the necklace. It landed in the sacking with the rest of the loot.

Julia reacted first, with the skill of an athlete born to make use of her opportunities. "Run!" she screeched at the top of her voice. She whipped the edger at Ausby, its sharp curve cleaving downward like a knife. Ausby's eyes widened, and he quickly ducked, but unfortunately for him, Julia's choice of weapon fell a little low. Its heavy metal handle cracked him solidly on one knee.

"Yow!" he yelled.

I grabbed the sacking with the stolen loot still inside and took off, Drew and Julia sprinting beside me. I chanced a backward glance, but Ausby was still cursing and trying to run after us with a hobbling gait. We tore across the soccer field.

"We can't go to my house!" I gasped. "He can't find out where I live!"

"We'll ditch him first," Drew puffed, "and then we'll circle around and go back to your house through the alley."

"He'll expect that," Julia objected. She looked back. "He's coming."

We put on a burst of speed. I clutched the sack with both hands, afraid that the fragile fabric wouldn't stay together. As we darted across the street, a familiar van pulled around the corner and stopped.

The van's window rolled down. "Izzy!" my mother's voice was sharp. "Get in here. Did you forget you had a game?"

We climbed inside, and shut and locked the door. The three of us were wheezing and breathless, but my mother had no time for that. She pulled away from the curb just as Richard Ausby made it to the edge of the park. He scowled after us. I collapsed into the backseat and buckled my seatbelt.

"What were you thinking?" she scolded. "First of all, the park is closed. Why were you in *there*? And you knew you had soccer—I reminded you this morning. I left your soccer bag right by the closet. What else do I have to do, send up smoke signals? For goodness sake, Iz. You have to get organized. It's a good thing you left me that note telling me where you were."

No kidding, I thought. "Did you bring my stuff?" I asked automatically.

Mom cast me a withering glance in the rearview mirror. "Yes, your bag is in the back. Julia, your mother is bringing your uniform to the game. You girls will have to get changed once we get there. And Drew, your dad called looking for you. You'd better call him back and tell him I'll drop you off at the game." Mom held her cell phone up.

"Thanks, Mrs. MacAllister," Drew said.

"Mom, there's something we need to do first—" I said.

"I don't want to hear it, Izzy. I didn't count on having to drive around for twenty minutes looking for you. I still have work to finish up at home, your game starts in five minutes, and no one has eaten supper, so don't even *suggest* that there's something else I have to do."

"But Mom, it's really important—"

"Sorry, Iz. But unless your hair is on fire, I'm not listening." Mom pulled into the parking lot without slowing down. Our team was hosting this game, so we were using an alternate field that Coach had managed to dig up. Mom braked hard. "Lucky for all of us, this field was only about ten blocks away. Have a good game. I'll try to get back to watch the second half. Have fun."

I stashed the old sacking full of loot in my soccer bag and leaped out of the van. I slammed the door shut just as Mom pulled away.

"Well, that's just great. Now what?" Julia said.

"Now we go play soccer," I said. "I put the stuff in with my gear. We'll go to the police right after the game. Ausby doesn't know where to find us. And how would anybody steal something out of my bag, when it's piled up with everyone else's and in plain sight? Besides, Drew can keep an eye on things.

"I don't know, Iz. I think we should tell my dad," said Drew.

"Me too," I agreed. "But do you really think he's going to listen now, right before the game? He's going to think we're from outer space. There's no way we can tell him in the next five minutes everything that's happened. And what then? Is he going to call off the game? No. All these parents and the other team would have to be told what's going on. No, I say we wait. It's a lot simpler. That stolen loot has been hidden for nearly a century. Another few hours aren't going to change anything."

"I guess you're right," Drew said. "I just don't like it, that's all."

"Me neither," Julia added.

"Girls!" Coach shouted across the parking lot. "Let's go! You're late!"

Drew ran across to the field, while Julia and I found her mother and the keys to their van so we could change. When I pulled out my uniform, an odd musty smell hit me. I wrinkled my nose and peered inside my soccer bag.

"Uh-oh," I said.

chapter nineteen

"What's wrong?" Julia asked.

"The trash is in here too."

"What trash?" Julia yanked her jersey over her head.

"From Ausby's place. Remember? You hid it in my bag." I thought for a minute. "Could I leave it in here?"

"In the van?" Julia shook her head. "I don't think so. My mom has a meeting. What if she finds it? She'll just throw it out."

"We can't risk that," I said. "It's the only evidence we have."

"Just bring it. We're really late." Julia popped open the sliding door. I yanked my jersey on and carefully grabbed my bag, now that I knew I had both the loot *and* the evidence.

At the field, Coach was pacing impatiently. "Where the heck have you two been?" he demanded. "The game's already started. Stretch and get ready to go out. I'll put you on the third shift."

I caught Drew's eye and deliberately placed my soccer bag in the center of everyone else's. Drew nodded and moved a little closer. Then I saw something that made my blood freeze. Richard Ausby was standing among the parents of the opposing team. He must have gotten in his own car and followed my mother's van to the game. I was also pretty sure he must have seen where I put my soccer bag. It wouldn't take a genius to guess that the loot was inside—most people don't hide their sports gear like they're protecting the crown jewels.

"Isabella! You're up!" bellowed Coach. The rest of my shift was already on the field. I didn't even have time to warn Drew that Ausby was here.

I galloped onto the field, joining my team as the game continued. It was hard to keep an eye on Ausby and the ball at the same time. Twice I lost the ball to the other team as I glanced at the sidelines to see where Ausby was. Coach paced like a caged lion. I could practically see him foaming at the mouth. When I flubbed a pass, giving it to the other team, I heard Coach groan. My face flamed as their star player raced through our defense, dodging and weaving with the ball stuck to her foot like glue. She fired a shot right at the net, but Ashley dove, grabbing the ball with her outstretched hands. Ashley booted the ball back in play. Julia took the pass and tore up the field.

"Izzy! Heads up!" Julia yelled, sending me a sizzling pass.

Stopping the ball with one foot, I looked where Julia was now pointing. Richard Ausby was striding purposefully along the sidelines, a black soccer bag in his hands—my soccer bag. Drew was nowhere to be seen.

I was frantic. If I yelled, Ausby was sure to run. He had to skirt the edge of the field in order to get to the parking lot, where I was sure he was headed. I had only one weapon— the soccer ball.

The timing had to be split-second. I would only have one chance. Perspiration slicked my palms. If ever I had to perform under pressure, this was it.

I dribbled the ball toward the sidelines, crossing over to the far corner. Our forward looked dumbfounded as I turned and, instead of taking a shot at the goal, began slowly backtracking along the sideline.

"Izzy, what are you doing? Play your position!" Coach hollered.

Ausby glanced up at the commotion, but before he could react I had worked myself into the spot I needed. I came at him head-on as he reached the edge of the spectators. I kept my sights on the soccer bag. Before my nerves could crumble I pulled my foot back and blasted off a shot with every ounce of strength I had.

The ball catapulted through the air with the precision of a missile. Ausby gripped the soccer bag and tried to run, which was a mistake. I'd been aiming for the bag, but now the target had moved. The ball walloped him right in the gut.

"Whoof!" Ausby gasped as the air rushed out of his lungs. He bent forward, struggling to breathe. I raced forward and snatched my soccer bag out of his hands.

"Drew!" I shrieked. "Coach! Someone call the police!"

Ausby tried to take a step forward, but without oxygen he was completely immobilized.

Coach and Julia pushed forward.

"Izzy! What were you thinking? Sir, are you all right?" Coach said, putting his hand on Ausby's shoulder.

"Don't!" I yelled. "He's a criminal. He tried to steal a valuable necklace, and he's the one who's been poisoning the soil at our soccer field."

"What!" Coach pulled back as though a snake had bitten him. "Are you sure?"

"Yes!" Julia and I exclaimed together.

"That's not true!" Ausby croaked, getting some of his wind back at last.

"Oh, yeah?" I challenged. "Then how can you explain walking off with this?" I opened my soccer bag. The sacking had come loose, and I drew out the ruby necklace with a flourish. The sight of it, gleaming with heavy jewels, drew gasps from the parents and players who were now clustered around.

Coach's jaw dropped. "Where did you get this?" he asked me.

"It was buried in an old root cellar on the property where our soccer field is," I answered.

"Property that *my* family owned. I didn't steal anything. Those jewels rightfully belong to me," Ausby said.

"No, they don't. They belong to whoever owns the land. And that's the city," Julia said.

"Not anymore," Ausby said with a smirk. "Your mother drew up the offer and I signed it this morning. I am buying that land back—land that should have been left to me in the first place."

That stopped me, but only for a moment. "What about the fact that those jewels were stolen in the first place?"

"The courts would have a hard time proving that," Ausby said smoothly. "After all, that train robbery was a long time ago."

"What train robbery?" Coach said.

"Okay, well, what about the contaminated soil?" I countered.

"What about it?" Ausby replied with an oily smile. "There was a lot of lead paint dumped there in the old days. Makes it unsafe for kids to play. I'm prepared to buy the land and clean it up."

"I just bet you are," I said grimly. "Because you would never have a chance to buy the land unless it *wasn't* fit for the public. Your great aunt wanted that land left for a recreation area. So you've been dumping lead out there and then complaining to the city."

"That's quite an accusation, young lady," Ausby snapped. "Considering you have no way to prove it."

I smiled. "Oh, but I do." I reached inside and drew out the Ziploc bag containing the jar with the metallic residue. "I think the police won't have any problem proving that this jar—which came from your trash—is coated with lead. Not to mention the printout we have that gives instructions on how to make sugar of lead."

Ausby's face was mottled purple, and his eyes narrowed with rage. He made a furious grab for the Ziploc bag. Coach caught his arm and held it down.

"Hey, now," he cautioned.

Ausby drew back his fist. "Back off, pal," he snarled. "I'm armed, but I don't want to use it. Make the little girl give me the bag, and I'll be on my way. If you don't, there's going to be a whole bunch of people hurt here today."

Coach stared at Ausby steadily. Then he swallowed. "Izzy, give him the soccer bag."

"But Coach, no—!" I protested.

"Do it, Isabella," Coach said. "It's not worth someone's life."

"He's right." Ausby scowled at me. "Give me the bag."

I hesitated.

"Now!" Ausby's voice sharpened.

Slowly, I took the soccer bag, dropped the evidence inside and held it out. But just as Ausby reached for it, the shrill wail of a siren cut the air. I jerked my hand back, still gripping the bag's handle, as a police truck roared into the parking lot. A police officer and a large dog jumped out. Ausby began to run.

The officer yelled a harsh command and the dog took off. Ausby let out a screech, and within seconds the dog had him pinned to the ground.

"Call him off! Call him off!" Ausby cried. The dog kept his jaws clamped over Ausby's forearm, growling.

The officer uttered another abrupt command and the dog let go. It backed off, but it still eyed Ausby with vicious hunger. I had no doubt it thought that Ausby would make a delicious meal.

Ausby must have had the same thought, because he offered no resistance when the officer handcuffed him.

"So, where's the kid?" the officer asked.

"What kid?" Coach, Ausby and I asked at the same time.

"The kid who phoned in a panic because he was locked in somewhere, and this guy was about to walk off with thousands of dollars worth of stolen goods," the officer answered.

"Drew!" I shouted.

"Where's my son?" Coach's face paled.

Before Ausby could answer, I heard a faint pounding coming from across the field, in the direction of the baseball diamond. The door of the porta-potty, which was fastened to the chain link fence, burst open at last, and Drew exploded from the interior, gasping for breath.

"Man!" he breathed as he reached us. "The smell in there nearly killed me. I thought I was a goner for sure!"

chapter twenty

"Why were you hiding in the porta-potty, anyway?" I asked. I dumped the mesh bag of soccer balls on the practice field. The yellow signs and caution tape had been removed, and I looked with pleasure at the familiar sight of our field.

"I wasn't hiding. I told you that," Drew answered. "Ausby told this little girl he wanted to play a joke on me and gave her five bucks to tell me that her brother was stuck in the outhouse. When I went over to help, Ausby jumped out from behind it, shoved me inside and jammed the door shut. None of you could hear me calling for help when the game was on. Everyone was making too much noise. It was lucky I had my cell phone."

"So you called the cops, but you never told them where you were," I said.

"I was more worried about Ausby getting away with the loot. Besides, who wants to get rescued from a porta-potty? That would look really great on the evening news!" Drew grimaced. "It was disgusting, but I knew I'd get out eventually."

"And now, Ausby's in jail, the park is safe, and we can get back to training for playoffs," I said. "Turns out he was in debt up to his eyeballs. Julia's mom found out when she did the offer for him on the land."

"I heard that was a pretty awesome kick you delivered, stopping Ausby like that," Drew said.

I blushed. "Luck," I answered.

"Not what I heard." Drew put both hands on my shoulders. "You can do it, Izzy. That was the ultimate. If you can hit Ausby with a ball under that kind of pressure, getting it past a goalie will be easy. I don't think you'll ever fall apart during a game again."

I thought about it, and a smile spread across my face. I knew he was right.

Michele Martin Bossley is the author of *Jumper*, also in the Orca Sports series. She lives in Calgary, Alberta.

Titles in the Series

orca sports

orca sports

For more information on all the books
in the Orca Sports series, please visit
www.orcabook.com.